This Little Tiger book belongs to:

_____

_____

_____

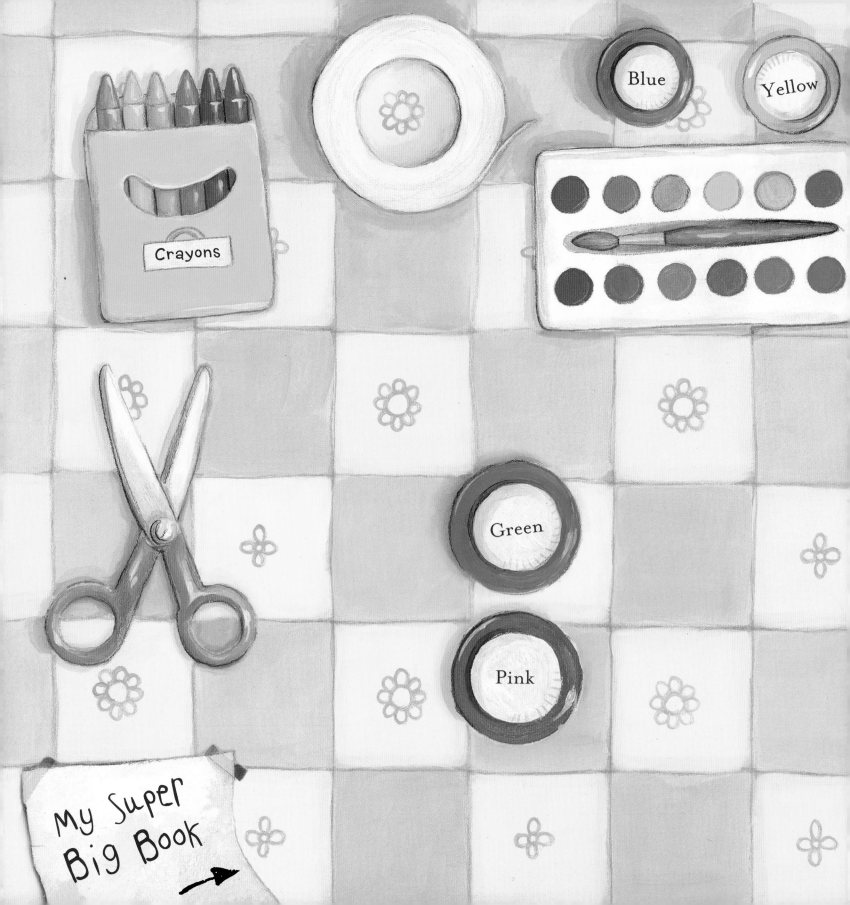

For Charlotte, with all my love xx ~ T C

For my cousin Felicity ~ A E

LITTLE TIGER PRESS LTD,
an imprint of the Little Tiger Group
1 The Coda Centre, 189 Munster Road,
London SW6 6AW
www.littletiger.co.uk

First published in Great Britain 2012
This edition published 2016

ISBN 978-1-84869-466-8
Printed in China
LTP/1800/1901/0417
2 4 6 8 10 9 7 5 3 1

Just One More!

Tracey Corderoy   Alison Edgson

LITTLE TIGER PRESS
London

Teatime was over. Bath time was over.
That meant just one thing . . .
   "Story time!" cried Little Brown Bunny.
   So Mummy read him a story.
Then another. Then *another*!

"Just *one* more," begged Little
Brown Bunny.

So Daddy read him one more story, right to the end.

Still Bunny said, "Just one more?"

"Granny's turn!" cried Daddy Rabbit.

When Granny had read *all* the dragon books,

and Grandpa had read them *again*, Little Brown Bunny still wanted . . . "Just one more!"

Mummy Rabbit gave a great big yawn.

"But Little Brown Bunny, look!" she said. "We've read all your stories, see? No more stories means it's time for sleep."

"Oh," said Bunny.

"Maybe," he whispered,
"I'll *make* a bedtime book.
A super, super-long one!
Then story time will last
all night."

Next morning Bunny hopped out of bed.
  "Hooray!" he cried. "Time to make
my story."

He bounced across to his making-things box.
Soon he was writing big, long words and
drawing lots of pictures.

At last, he heaved up his heavy book.
This was going to be the longest
story *ever*!

"Are you sitting comfortably?"
he asked his toys. "We might be here
a long, long time!"

Two minutes later, it was all over.
"MU-U-UM!" called Bunny.
"My super-long story wasn't
super-long at all."

"Don't worry," said Mum. "Why don't you go and ask your friends what stories *they* like? Then you can add them to your book."

"Clever Mummy!" cried Little Brown Bunny, and off he went.

CARROT
COTTAGE

Little Owl was playing with his rocket
when Bunny bounced in.

"*My* favourite stories," he hooted, "are
ones about the moooooon! One day I'm
going to fly there! Zooooom!"

"I love the moon, too!" said Bunny.

"Thanks, Owl!"

And he blasted off to find Little Mouse . . .

Little Mouse was having a teeny snack when Bunny bounded in. "I love stories about cheese!" she mumbled. "Big cheese, small cheese, round cheese, pongy cheese – *any* cheese really!"

"Thanks, Mouse!" giggled Bunny, holding his nose. And he raced off to find Little Wolf . . .

Little Wolf was having a tea party when
Bunny came by.

"Well, I do love stories about piggies!"
he said. "And that grandma with the big,
furry ears!"

"*My* favourite story," grinned
Big Daddy Wolf, "is the one
all about . . ."

"Hugs!"

"Oh, Daddy," giggled
Little Wolf, "what big
arms you have!"
"All the better to hug
you with!" chuckled
Daddy Wolf. And
he gave his boy
a big daddy kiss
on the nose.

"Thanks for your help," Bunny
called. Then he huffed and puffed
all the way back home!

Little Brown Bunny got out his book and scribbled down stories of moons made of cheese, and rockets and big, fluffy hugs.

By the time he had finished, it was dark outside.

"Come on, everyone!" he called. "This is going to be the best, most super-duper storybook *ever*!"

He opened it ever so
carefully and took a big,
deep breath. Then Little
Brown Bunny . . .

. . . fell fast asleep!

Mummy is reading Little Brown Bunny
his favourite bedtime stories.
"*Just one more!*" he cries.
But there are no stories left!
So Little Brown Bunny has
a wonderful idea . . .

Little Tiger Press

ISBN 978-1-84869-466-8

90100>

9 781848 694668

£6.99

www.littletiger.co.uk

The Useless Troll

Written by
Alec Sillifant

Illustrated
by
Joëlle
Dreidemy